Roses are READ
Love lost or found

Timothy G. Green

Roses are Read - Love lost or found

ISBN 978-0-9822796-0-1

Editors: Mary Mitchell - marymitchell139@yahoo.com

Kishuana Ross - Kishuana.ross11@gmail.com

Cover Design: Donna Osborn Clark at CreationsByDonna@gmail.com

Layout and Interior Design: Creative Unity Productions

Published by: **INKaissance Books**
inkaissance@gmail.com

INKaissance Books

This book is dedicated to everyone who embraces
L.O.V.E. to its highest degree:
Loyalty Over Virtually Everything

Introduction

Nostalgia

The flame of my penmanship
seeks redemption to feast from the fire,
that can only be set ablaze by many days
of boldly riding the horse & carriage
of poetic aspire...

Crying mercy while awaiting the grasp of a hand
is this one lonely feeble pencil,
with its eraser beheaded, stature blinded and dismal,
even microphones capture the breath
of poets & playwrights during recitations,
open mic nights & slam venues
become victims of an arrested nation...

Thoughts begin to surface and arise
of blatant sabotage,
as a poignant arrogance seduces the
minds of many poets to accept this mirage,
of vanquishing the poetic art
through envious camouflage;
raising the question of what is love?

Flirtatiously I scribe on my notepad
through the seduction of my pencil,
my deepest thoughts release
at a rapid pace from within my mental.

With gratitude, sincerity and genuine purpose
calmly I begin to tickle her surface,
reciting to her words with a mystique allure
innovative and creative - colorful like a circus.

One thing is for certain,
when I see the grand opening
of the stages curtain,
my spirit vastly begins yearning,
anxiously to taste the nectar like aura
from the microphone it's been desperately thirsting...

Hypnotized as I grab her, my pupils offset and stagger...
My voice deepens - openly admitting that my lungs
are having a difficult time breathing...

My soul reclines cemented,
for it's never engaged
in love making so authentic...

In order to encompass her affectionate beauty and kindred nature
I had to first grab my paintbrush, well my favorite pencil,
and release the deepest thoughts
from my soul on a piece of paper...

That's where it all started because Roses are Read.

Table of Contents

She loves me, she loves me not

Timothy G. Green

She loves me...

Without hesitation I would trade my life for yours,
honorably petition the gate keepers of heaven
to allow you through heavens doors,
trust in God will conquer fear as our love matures,
as He equips and orders our steps in preparation
of walking on Kingdom floors...

She loves me not...

Believing in finding true love seems so past tense,
the last alleged true love broke my heart
and I haven't laughed ever since,
I walk jealous because my cheeks and eyes make love
every day through a seductive rinse,
I yearn for this experience with a woman
yet I feel summoned by incompetence,
for I have allowed past relationships to destroy my confidence...

She loves me...

Poetically astounded, I venture to taste the fruit
of the root in which love was founded...
I'm willingly ready to put my guard down,
even restructure my smile that is often
embarked with a bitter frown,
I'm simply a King in search of a Queen to secure
my spirits hallowed crown,
as I in return would teach her growth and patience
through my actions,
freedom by all means necessary,
never attempting to keep her barred down...

Roses are Read

She loves me not...

It's very likely that you don't even like me,
your eyes, stature and mouth have yet to invite me...
for a conversation; as if your hearts freedom
is now captive within a depressed conquered nation...
Your very slow to answer me... That must be it...
I already knew it,
our hearts can never stand congruent,
you're already taken!

She loves me...

With an expectant spirit I trust destiny
to ultimately prevail,
if I could script my love life,
I would scribe it in supreme detail,
I'm open to selling out for love,
but not in the form of posturing like retail,
my goal is to enroll our soul's in heaven,
opposite from residing in hell,
deeply I inhale, for this is a love story
I would be honored to forever re-tell...
She loves me not...
Every other day it seems that you drown me
in tales of deceit,
and as I continue to take steps forward
in faith towards you -
you continue to be selfish and put yourself first,
from my love you retreat,
together we are untouchable, united, victorious...
never facing defeat,
divided we have no value like a lost receipt...
No proof of love between us ever existing!

Timothy G. Green

She loves me...

The symbolism of roses magnifies
your heart and encloses,
favored vibes that prescribe
the pureness of love in heavy doses,
I honor our bond and the brawn of our closeness...

She loves me not...

How could you ever truly love me
yet verbally exploit my every flaw,
I came to bring justice in your life,
but you blatantly play the outlaw,
I enrolled in your heart with no plans to ever withdraw,
but I'm suffering from being frost bitten –
so I bid you good ridden
as I allow my mind, body, & soul
ample time to un-thaw...
Sincerely,

Confused hearted

Humbly Honoring
Hearts Horizon

With tears of innocence her cheeks became flooded,

my young love is truly warm blooded,

evident from her kindred spirits welcoming of my

soul, as it was harmlessly approached

and with sovereignty confronted.

Ever so delicate was my poetic etiquette...

I astonished, with a loving promise to

the angels of heavens summit,

as I thanked God in advance

for the future womb that would consume

much room in her stomach,

a heart predestined and unquestioned

to sing graceful melodies with a steady drumming,

for this newborns love will be written

by the winds from which it has been summoned,

to grow as a pillar and carry our

family name forward.

Eye cry for you

My tears serenade upon your soul
as it melts like butter,
removing charred scars to a place a far,
so that your heart may be uncovered,
love discovered as cherubs silently began to hover,
over our thoughts so that they may be caught
with an aura of peace...

My words release like a dove that has been
imprisoned in a cage,
freely searching for love,
as sultry winds set my wings ablaze,
I peck on the sun so that upon it
my past wounds may be engraved,
as God grants those burdens serenity by releasing
them through sun rays...

I offer you freedom sweetheart that is rooted
like a stalwart sequoia,
more than lecture, I respect your inner beauty,
admiring its architecture...
Your body is your temple,
just as the God in you
mentors your mental,
for you are a kindred spirit...
with a smile colorful as a parrot;
humbly my lungs drum to the ballad
of your love's instrumental...

As I swallow more than my pride but also all
of my selfish motives,
denounced ounce by ounce,
even by the gallon in immense doses,
without hesitation I have sworn to swallow
the thorns of 5 dozen roses,
so for the first 60 days I speak
this past pain shall remain closest,
to my breath...

Roses are Read

I vow to swallow the weight of your sorrow,
perched upon my shoulders as if I were Apollo...
I swallow a Godly fluid to abolish the loneliness
which enslaves your heart
with depressed feelings of existing hollow...

I swallow, loving you as if you are mine today
cosigned by love yesterday,
and shall continue to be especially tomorrow,
by example my love is setting to lead,
praying that you follow...

Timothy G. Green

The surface of my heart

Roses are Read

Only one mention of my goal releases virtues so true,

Thus, slowly the extension of my soul

reaches out to you...

It is evident from the wings perched upon your back

that you are heaven sent,

Even the aura of your characters decor is blossomed

with a sweet heaven scent,

My sole intent is to assure the foundation

of our spiritual nourishment,

Through guidance fueled by love, faithfulness

& Godly encouragement,

If your heart is empty my love please grant me

permission to furnish it,

with loyalty inspired by graceful

will and genuine gestures

blessed ever so righteous, Godly and firmament...

The alluring scintillation in your eyes

flirtatiously hint to me,

that you are a woman of highest moral

with standards resolutely set on victory,

Specifically my poetry stimulates a celestial intimacy,

because I honor "not self" in my work

but humbly He...

Love, patiently I await for your heart to cross

the threshold of my soul's gate,

please trust the echoing voice lingering in your soul

and allow cupids arrow to deeply penetrate...

Together we are destined to rise,

above the lows and beyond the highs,

set to soar with authority within heavens skies,

soul to soul we scream love as our hearts compromise,

the world watches our authenticity as we capture their eyes,

the clouds wink with a glimpse of the sun

whispering to them

TRUE LOVE NEVER DIES,

the eye of the storm is calm - the eye of the owl is wise,

this lonely soul is on the road to recovery

no longer shall you hear her cries...

UPON THE SURFACE OF MY HEART

Next lifetime

Timothy G. Green

Thoughts arranged in a manner indecisive
allows temptation to enter my inner
with savory mental injections which entices...

My calm stature to abandon its poise
sought lust and once found
the humblest spirit can be destroyed...

I mean, don't get me wrong, but I seek to over stand
that my sincere love for you
first has you impregnated,
before we attempt to enter parenthood
unbalanced and stagnated...

Hear my cry, hear my plea, and hear the splatters
of my soul as it bleeds,
touch my heart, cover my eyes, but please hear the
splatters of my soul as it bleeds...
I vowed to secure not your wants but your every need,
as the man I accepted my oath to lead,
but first we must ensure that
our sacred garden of trust
in one another is fertile before we can
commence in harvesting seeds...

How could you leave and abandon our loves ship?
I had no life jacket within my reach;
slowly I drown in my tears,
soul now handcuffed and imprisoned by despair,
the realm of lost love,
I now reside in its bottomless pit...

The sweltering heat of this desert
burns my soles to my soul,
the voiceless wind ignores my every
request of reconciliation,
for it seems there is no cure for
these mental abrasions...

14

Roses are Read

Yet, as I venture on and find a cactus I use its quills
to send you one last message,
I scribe your name within my veins
so my *undying love for you*
can defeat your every pain...

I release this same cactus from bondage
and lay it flat on its back...
Painfully fitting it is, as upon it my sore body
it perfectly overlaps...
A pair of sandstorms form and simultaneously
release a thunderous clap,
as my pupils swallow this mirage, slowly they elapse...

I kneel as my soul finally is able
to make peace with what seems to be death,
Painfully yearning for a taste of true love...

My child, awaken...

The earth beneath my lifeless body has been visibly shaken,
He kept His word to never leave me
thank You Father for I was definitely not forsaken...

I lived solely for this person, loved solely for this person,
and that is the reason why, my child, that your soul needs nursing,
argument after argument, even after being hit, I never hit back or
resorted to cursing,
but you failed to acknowledge the signs that over the years their anger only worsened,
and you inadvertently began to idolize them, for My love, you were no longer thirsting,
so all along it was act on their part, for the ending to come they were
simply rehearsing?
Yes, they were disguised as an heaven sent Angel,
radiating an imitation light the bore the same glow,
now tell me, when did you ever see darkness overtake a rainbow,
or what is said to be love only inflict anger, bitterness, and hate so painful,
I gave you plenty of signs to leave but you comfortably continued to sit in the same row,
you willfully excepted stagnation when I taught you how to speak life and claim flow,
and now that you know, will you embrace this humility as healing and remain low;

Timothy G. Green

Will you?
This is the question my child that I truly must know...

I'm so ashamed to know that I was ready to submit and commit suicide,
because of the scintillating throbbing that was destroying me inside,
I was verbally abused me about my weight as if I were a genocide,
a poison to their very existence so by ignoring me intentionally
I was put in degrading mental and emotional positions to be crucified,
although with no hesitation for them I would have honorably died,
selfish is — selfish does
for every ounce of truth I shared I received
a gallon of words accented in lies,
where there is a lack of self accountability
then two hearts will always collide,
when they turned their back to me every time I cried,
I now know to thank You Father for those moments
for keeping my integrity and maturity beautified,
You instructed me to love myself from here on out
and with an obedient heart I promise to abide.

Remember my child to beware of those enter your life with the spirit of a python,
they slither in swiftly yet slowly begin to choke My presence out of you
and desire you to worship them like an icon,
we talk so much about the wolf in sheep's clothing but never about
the vulture disguised as a swan,
so verily, verily I say unto you
smile and rejoice from the sound of My voice
be wiser with the meditations of your heart and the consequences
that come with every choice,
as your next lifetime begins now...

Why me?

Timothy G. Green

I didn't always know how to show you my love thus
you had the right to question it,
I should have embraced your hand in marriage to
solidify my verbal vows as definite,
I miss how you cherished my heart and the many
times your peaceful thoughts would rest in it,
which tickled the border of my soul
so tender and affectionate...

To think of the time I spent with you
and how much of it I wasted,
to think of the countless times your smile quenched
my thirst and now I yearn once again to taste it,
I know my character is unorthodox;
far from being average or basic,
however please know when I cry - I humbly rely
on my tears to keep my spirit calm in its nature...

Still, I offer no excuses for my lack of commitment,
and respect your stance of
the cold shoulder and resentment.

Yet, you told me on my voice mail
that you knew I loved you,
from the first kiss I placed on your forehead
when I proudly hugged you,

Roses are Read

when you emptied your darkest secrets
within the brightest colors of my heart pallet
and I never judged you…

That alone adds a heavenly luster and celestial shine
to what my heart has to offer,
while I allow God to mend it with his merciful
fruits so that it may be refined,
Willingly this mountain of shame
I shall bravely climb,
attempting to surface my love
wholeheartedly once again
within the confines of your mind,
for it was we - not love that was truly blind;
perhaps...

Timothy G. Green

I breathe the nights today

Roses are Read

Dance with me on the sun's surface
as our body heat intensifies,
like the scintillating scorch of summer days in July.

The road upon which your weary feet travel
I relish its soil,
sculpting massive sand castles from it
for your touching of the earth ordained art as royal.

The compassionate delivery of your words
nurture my souls garden,
promising a golden harvest despite
the frigid stalking of the winter,
assuring ripe vegetation of maturity
& fruitful blessings of trust.

I stand beneath the pale moonlight
with my arms poised...

Reminiscent of the sun setting over the horizon,
my righteous heart is vastly crying,
yearning to crown you my Queen
over terrain righteous like Zion.

I honor the strength of your wisdom,
the voice of your judgment,
humbly I would allow my life to perish before yours
unto you I vow this devout covenant,
destiny permitted this oath to be scribed
deep within my soul,
as Heaven is the proprietor of its publishing...

I breathe the nights today

Timothy G. Green

The light within the tunnel

Roses are Read

I see the temperature rise in your eyes at a high rate,

as tears roll uneven down

your cheeks because they vibrate,

pupils purposely so pure could never lie straight,

so eye cry too in essence of this Angelic state,

no matter how far;

physically my love shall never migrate,

for spiritually we are;

rightful key holders to His golden gates.

Our fingers web like silk thread blessed by Charlotte,

so I remain focused on sewing these words

to your heart which is my

beloved and favorite garment,

your gentle likeness is the ripest with Cupid's market,

as your scarlet cheeks align rather divine

when I roll out the red carpet.

Righteously my cheeks posture like brownstone,

my heart nestles in your soul

like a newborn who has gracefully just arrived home,

humble am I that Heavens winds have allowed

this path to be shown,

that shall lead to my prayer being fulfilled by God

of not having to suffer by dying in this world alone.

Timothy G. Green

arisen from my hearts shadow

Roses are Read

May I please lay my head on your pillow?
Can the warmth of my soul comfort the misery
of your heart and persuade
it to embrace the rose; not its thorns?

Please allow my devotion to grow peacefully
within your hearts vessel,
so that it may flow freely through your body
and massage your veins.
As my hands interlock with your hands during prayer,
our sentiments to
the most high travel worry free,
perched on the wings of a dove...

As the candle centers our dinner table,
its light allows me to gaze into your soul...
Enabling my mind to be set free and sail afloat my tears
as they rejoice by streaming upon
your smiles radiant moonlight...

Every wink of your eye deposits trust in my heart
and increases its interest...
It's cupids arrow, which I pray will pierce your heart,
ever so gently my love.
Abstract, as we make love through reciting poetry,
stimulating electric waves
in our lungs which release an energy so potent,
it slightly tilts the earth's balance,
as I catch your Fall after the Autumn season...
If my undying love for you were a book, it would be page-less,
for I would simply
scribe my feelings everyday through
portrayal of courteous mannerisms unto you.

You see, I love my mother and she is no bitch,
so calling you out of your name
would only leave my honor for her in a state of discontent...

A vow made before God that I shall never break

Timothy G. Green

Whisper

Roses are Read

Secretly,
I know my name
is engraved deep within
your pupils lurking silently
amongst the boundaries
of their shadows...

The frustration
of simply not hearing
my name called by you
aspires attrition in my soul,
yet its flesh encompasses my
heart like the skin of an apple...

Rhythmically it orchestrates
the melodies of chimes
as they feverishly dance
with the wind.

When it finally travels
from your lungs and escapes
into air - it is then ordained,
not "my" but our beautiful name...
For the harmonious balance
its secular has maintained...

Timothy G. Green

Dear Sunset

Roses are Read

All for you my Queen,
my beloved Dearest Sunset,
I await tomorrows experience
to see if my heart shall
race the fastest race
it has run yet.

As you submerged within
the milky glazing
of the mountain slope,
it was the savory
melting of your buttery
accent which hinted
syrup to release from my eyes.

My breaded soul stood ardent,
thanking you for the toast.
Ye' blessed my garden,
cherry red tomatoes which
gave me strength to ketchup
to the sight of you drifting
slowly away.

Humbly I wave with
the ocean while bowing
my head with the trees.
I applaud in unison with
the thunderous claps of lightning;
praising your existence…

Lett-uce be grateful for
the "renaissance" restoration
of celestial scenery,
via the novel life you resurrected
upon the souls of your
admirers fading greenery,
in which the goddess fertility
has chosen to be her child.

Timothy G. Green

The gallantry of your character
shines radiance amongst we
when you awaken and arise,
amongst the throne of God
yet you surround yourself
with the faithful marshmallows
in the heavenly skies...

I await tomorrow's experience
to see if my heart shall
race the fastest race
it has run yet,
all for you my Queen,
my beloved Dearest Sunset.

One Memorable Breakfast

My eye lids peeled back as if I were undressing a banana. It was flirtatiously fruitful how our eyes met and instantly ripened our pupils. The radiant softness of your smile browned your cheeks like pancakes, as my heart melted upon them like butter.

Although my thoughts were scrambled like the eggs on your plate, I decided to slide over easy. My mind gave my heart a citrus tickle, inspiring me to freshly squeeze out my feelings for you, reminiscent of the Orange Juice that sat to the top right corner of your plate.

Graciously I buttered a toast in appreciation of your attire, which was very crisp like the strips of bacon that rested on top of your home fries. Whenever you spoke, sweetness released and poured from your lungs, like the packets of syrup you glazed your pancakes with. I didn't have a red carpet available so I had to improvise.

I dropped a napkin or two near your feet for you to walk across. My heart could not bear thoughts of your feet touching the sticky surface of the restaurants floor. Your smile tipped my soul as if I had served it. A meal well served this morning I'd say.

Check please... This one is on me!

OPEN HEART LETTER

Timothy G. Green

Forever beautiful is the sun within my heart
that you have set,
its warmth is vibrantly soothing as it poises my soul
to speak freely without fear
hesitation nor any feelings of regret.

You are a woman, Mother Nature to who man
is forever in debt,
I love the strength in which you build me and shield me as you
yield me from many of life's threats.

From my heart to yours, forever am I grateful of you...

Admirably I observe the will power of your grace and
respect your sense of friendship,
easily you reach me for I am not one to shy away
as you teach me;
Humbly I oblige to be your soulful apprentice.

Your beauty tickles my heart in a gentle
manner yet relentless,
so if I do not comply with your standards
then please exhibit your forgiveness,
and know that our combined efforts bring forth balance
and my loyalty towards you cannot die young for cupids arrow
pierced it with love endless.

From my heart to yours, forever am I grateful of you...

I know you can feel my heart stroking your heart
with the firmest of touches,
so carefully this entrancing pallet of yours
my inner spirit clutches,
as my undying love canvas your mind with God
blessing the very paint found on my brushes.
Allow me to be your comforter
as I honorably make adjustments;
to unlock your hearts desires.

Roses are Read

From my heart to yours, forever am I grateful of you...

I love you deeply and will always support you sincerely,
with the utmost of respect I yearn to feel the honesty of
your smile so close near me...

Please know these vows I sow are extended by cherubs
as I pray your spirit can hear me clearly,
for if ever given the opportunity please note
that I honorably shall carry...
these vows which I have expressed
through love, prayer and eyes joyfully teary!

From my heart to yours, forever am I grateful of you...

Timothy G. Green

Before my lungs collapsed...

Roses are Read

I invited you to travel with me to heaven
riding faith in the form of shooting stars
piloting a crescent...

Eye glazed the pinkest carnations with my tears
so my love could be mirrored unto your soul at every glance...
The salt within them would provide a nurturing fertility
molding its character through infinity,
through memory,
through recollections of our kinetic energy,
poetic was our chemistry; at least I thought...

To hell with cupid though
and his poisonous arrow,
which carried an artificial love
blackened like a sparrow,
seduced my soul with armored honesty as the apparel,
me being a sucker for love
altered my vision and I became a victim by way of deception
thus making my third eye narrow...

Easily I was led on, your lies - obliviously I fed on,
you walked out of my life, yet my heart bled on,
even though my love was bailed on,
I loved you unconditionally so my inner held on,
as I watched my heart take on a derailed form,
the eyes of my soul reigned over this frail storm,
they literally rained over this frail storm...
Regardless of the throe caused from our ageless clashes,
the countless times my soul was charred
unidentifiable to ashes,
the emotional scars my mind endured from engulfing
the barrage of your verbal acids,
the anger which arose within my soul chose to remain passive,
for love was birthed genuine,
thus, why couldn't our state of it be deemed as classic?

Timothy G. Green

I honored the deposit of love you filtered
in my heart like an ash tray,
along with my vow to mold, better yet sculpt our relationship
with perfection and divine understanding,
for its foundation was supported with mystique glass clay,
I forgave you, just as He forgave me,
at last my love
united you and I gracefully pray.

Human error is a symptom of life which one can never forsake,
for we all are entitled to making our fair share of mistakes,
over time many relationships are prone
to rumble like earth quakes,
yet, through exhibiting faith, they always have potential
to breath peace and life reflective of a great lake,
while inhaling success through the smoke our love creates...

Fall-ing in Love

Timothy G. Green

Poet tree rooted our love with an aroma of syrupy maple,
which leave when the leaves Fall
yet resurface with a Spring in the month of April,
painted in burnt auburn, cranberry crimson, and walnut hazel,
also flavored with a Christmas splash of pine tree basil,
that gently tap dance romance into every lovebirds nasal,
as Autumn winks in acceptance of this latest love appraisal.

The wind blows as leaves flow to the earth below reluctant,
from an Ariel view it appears they blanket
the earth in discomfort,
however many shine golden while others
are bronzed in mustard,
symbolically these leaves breathe the life of an orchard,
for they are off springs of this poet tree's
oxygen and especial moisture.

This poet tree also offers squirrels that literally
go nuts over girls,
bright eyed and bushy tailed as they are given love referrals,
just as the wise owls who script these love memoirs in journals,
in their mind during the day
for at night they seek love in the realm of the nocturnal.

For the story behind the Fall of this leaf
is truly needed inside of a man,
with the veins of the leaf outlining his hearts diagram,
so he can learn to poise and posture
himself in preparation of Fall-ing in love

Sleeping with the Angels

If my words can flow freely
like the tears escaping your eyes,
massaging the poetic mosaic
which encompasses your heart...

If my hands could cover
the eyes of your soul,
asketh do I that it judge me not
by sight but of spirited faith,
while traveling the path of my manhood
using a torch lit from the fiery furnace of my heart,
to guide ye - for it shall oblige thee
of being safe...

Yet, I whisper this prayer
perfecting perfect alignment,
of my eyes to be acute with Heavens horizon,
A plethora of saccharine rain drops
give birth from the sky and shower my aspirations,
golden is the colorization of this divine connotation...

My beloved Queen has finally awakened,
after a well deserved rest in which she has partaken,
while Sleeping with the Angels.

One step closer

Timothy G. Green

Laced with faith is the look upon your beautiful face,

amazed with grace am I for these steps

we are preparing to take,

one step closer to unity is this love of ours,

one step closer...

At the rapid pace that you have

consistently ran through my mind,

I always could foresee the day when we our hearts

would ultimately cross paths and tie the knot...

Marching down the aisle will uproot all traces of dirt

gathered on my soul...

Approaching the alter I calmly

release the strap from my tongue,

setting the tone for my voice to recite wedding vows...

As we step forward in the name of love we realize our destiny;

The shoe fits, so it's only fair that we wear it...

I DO...

YES, I DO ACCEPT THIS TRUE COME DREAM,

BUT DOES IT ACCEPT ME?

Shadowed by love

Timothy G. Green

I can hear your heart taking footsteps,
as my soul extends its arms to reach thee,
never shall I forsake the power of breath,
so I inhale hope in dire attempt as I beseech thee,
many puddles have been created from the tears I have wept,
may they comfort your fruitful spirit and ripen its peach tree,
if your love, which I cherish were to perish,
then I'd have nothing left,
for it is from the fountain of your tears which I drink,
only its nectar has the strength to increase me...

The fog thickens, prompting my heartbeat to quicken,
thoughts of not finding you encompass my soul as it sickens,
despite lacking light my soul chooses to recite an invite,
through an array of "my heart is open" poetic renditions...

Visions insisting I reminisce although the winds scream brisk,
knowing the locking of our lips shall bring
forth a celestial eclipse,
my vision gets interrupted
for the wind has fortified its scream of brisk...

Briefly my soul hears your echoes urging I not to let go,
although eye cannot see you, your words
clutch my inner like Velcro,
soothing is this whisper that simmers sweet as cocoa,
willingly I allow my faith to board its
vessel and embark upon its flow,
now present is your scent of aloe
which paces my love to hasten its paddles,
I feel it is only a matter of time before
I engulf my Queens shadows,
until misery intervenes and cast fear within
my throat through seditious lasso's,
contaminating my breath - eroding the grains of my flesh,
I kneel in sacrifice to life until
your light emancipates my death...

Roses are Read

The discharge of this soulful cry beckons cherubs
to part heavens skies,
a sign of serenity from He, as His disciples,
our brethren humbly comply, in peaceful relief
you release a sigh,
it harmonizes a familiar melody,
one in which thy angels gracefully fly...

I now realize to possess true love one has to allow self to die,
while trusting the process of love no matter the distance,
to selflessly reply.

Timothy G. Green

Charred Imperfections

Roses are Read

As the gasoline within your tears poured upon my love letter,
the synergy of the heat within it instantly ignited,
releasing smoke signals of distress in heavens direction.

As fumes arose, dense fog made its presence known,
cupid's vision was altered as his arrow missed your hearts
mark by the narrowest of margins,
yet just enough to blur your hearts ear drums
from hearing my soul's plea...

Helplessly, my thoughts disintegrated before my eyes,
napkins were sown to my pupils like aprons
as they absorbed the anguish.

The flesh of my words burned to ashes,
drifting slowly in your direction,
you were able to only catch a partial glimpse of them
a third of their initial reflection...

Yet, my love letters furnace still fueled an undying flame,
so I crumbled a hand full of its ashes into bread crumbs
and carefully placed them in your mouth to digest,
hoping their fiery infernal would brand
your tongue, lungs and throat with my love infinitely...

So whenever you would speak my love would be released,
so whenever your saliva would leak
a glaze over the dimples of your cheeks,
my lips would be there spiritually to meet them at their peak,
my love letter would assure your breath
of not becoming faint or weak
for my love would be released whenever you chose to speak...

Upon your soul a love emblem scarred,
ravishing though, with the twinkle of the universe's stars,
riding the comet of loyalty despite
being imperfect and charred.

Timothy G. Green

Will you deposit?

Roses are Read

I assure you that there's no need of false questioning,

as you conduct my love's background

check when cross referencing,

for in your heart I truly see value and this check

shall not bounce,

for I am fully aware of the repercussions of having

my reputation tarnished and denounced,

I am guilty of depositing my love in large amounts,

and losing my interest in 90% of these offshore accounts,

many of these investors were guilty of theft of identity,

for on the outside they promoted

their loyalty with positive imagery,

but once my account was set up their

intentions were shown vividly,

as they unbalanced the majority of my love investment books

and made me the enemy,

I was shocked because I was always willing to make change

and more than money – I had time to spend,

but they were solely more interested in my initial dividends,

I was a fool to accept their sale pitch

which started this tragedy,

for their words were very cunning

while humming with flattery,

as I was second nature to my financial salary,

Yet I hope you find it within your hearts

bank to give me a chance

although my faith in love is largely in debt,

I am not currency driven or imprisoned

so please my dear invest,

review my financial statements from my past love in depth,

and embrace with haste

the opportunity to restore spiritual air

back to its rightful place...

MY BREATH

thee outpour of love

Timothy G. Green

It was her choice, to release jazz notes of love from her voice,

in the form of heavens boardwalk,

painted in hues of turquoise,

we then decide to ride this high

classy - renting from heaven a Rolls Royce,

As the eyes of our storm release rain

upon our cheeks terrain ever so moist,

rejoice do us folks, flirtatiously blowing kisses,

through perfected brush strokes,

shelled hearts now unyoke, no longer eschewed to barter hope,

mere words expressed through sheer herbs

enticed like the aroma of grilled artichokes,

darker smokes are merely uttered,

charcoal would only distract my feelings

for you that are buttered,

pouring from the tip of my tongue,

is the thickness of my love's enrichment, similar to mustard,

hoping the unorthodox flow of my souls pallet

can be seen as valid and keep your heart fluttered...

Roses are Read

this drop of tear is a very rare figment of my imagination,

filled with glares that are pigments of my infatuation,

poured upon my smock with no degree of separation,

for when our hearts are acquainted

the love is sincerely painted,

in dire respiration...

dire respiration...

dire respiration...

dire respiration...

Timothy G. Green

Undeniable

Roses are Read

When I first saw you I was afraid to speak...

When I finally spoke I was afraid to hear your response...

When I heard your response I began to like you...

By the grace of God you began to like me too...

Naturally life took its course and we fell in love...

Now that we are in love I am so afraid to lose you...

But are you afraid to lose me?

Take me away

Roses are Read

The curiosity in your stare is the bait,

my heart bites and falls directly into your pupils web,

your insight over flows, water falls from this waterfall,

flooding my manhood with an agape cleansing,

as your morals stand firm,

nurturing mankind is scribed with His blood

on your souls tablet,

raising me to approach life's pulpit and question it...

How can a star stare into space when her

breath of life is universal?

Hypnotized by your speech as intuitive

thoughts release each time,

my ambition extracts into a metamorphosis,

a butterfly net, as I vigorously try to capture your wisdom,

wishing I could sleep walk over the piano keys of your mental,

or have the privilege of bathing in your hearts fireplace.

With you my heart is never overwhelmed

with emotion or distress,

you give sight to my once blinded search for love,

penetrating deep within the creases of my hearts vessels,

so I can taste the purity of your divinity in my veins,

with wind so calm it settles,

upon the softest palms as it nestles...

Sweetness, yes for it my soul has a weakness,

I need not ask of your permission to share with you

more of my life's secretes.

Timothy G. Green

In the midst of life's turmoil

where I fail you effortlessly excel,

where I thirst for knowledge of life like a hungered fetus

you continually refill your intuitions well,

beneath loves surface I crawl

above heaven's terrain you freely dwell,

even upon cupid's tears I float

yet, across cupid's tears you humbly sail.

Soulful is this circumcision of falling in love with you,

the texture is smooth as silk yet very durable like denim,

love is love as a captive in your hearts prism,

those who did you wrong in the past, do not fret, I forgive em,

they have taught me to respect you in Beethoven's rhythm,

nothing less than exceptional, far more than sexual,

attracted am eye to thy intellectual, the fruit of thy labor,

my harvested jewel...

Take me away!

STOP

Timothy G. Green

STOP making excuses for his disrespect,

STOP believing your only outlet is to suffer in his neglect,

STOP using his love for your children as a reason,

STOP being his sponge to soak his anger upon

so that his knuckles may cry by bleeding,

STOP thinking you need that man in your life to survive,

when he hasn't been there to witness how you overcame many

struggles in your life before him

your testimony is that the Most High

has blessed you to still be alive!

STOP thinking the solution to your problems with him

is to engage in marriage,

when he cannot even man up to attempt to cleanse

his own eroded spirit...

STOP feeling sympathetic for his verbal abuse,

that often leads to his hands tightening around

your neck like a noose,

STOP putting your love for him over your own child,

before you become permanently blind

Roses are Read

to the scars hidden beneath your child's smile...

STOP thinking short skirts and tight jeans

are needed to attract every mans affection,

when that one night stand can lead to death

without the use of protection...

STOP wishing death upon yourself

when he walks out your life,

instead use those tears to wipe your soul

clean and garner a new sight...

STOP wanting the world to accept your pain and offer charity,

instead look deep into your souls mirror carefully,

see the beautiful Queen you are destined

to become with clarity,

and trust not him, but Him, to lead you to greater prosperity...

STOP gossiping on others when your own life isn't stable,

pierce not your navel or your tongue with a ring

but with God's word because to do exceedingly and abundant

only He is truly able.

Timothy G. Green

STOP lying, STOP crying, STOP submitting to slowly dying,

STOP denying your chance of living a prosperous life

and instead START trying...

WOMEN OF THE WORLD WE NEED YOU

Through the crack of a confession

Timothy G. Green

I toast this glass of poetry in your honor,

through this confession I humbly

camera my cerebration's to your soul...

I plead with you to understand

why I'm only giving you flashes,

for I am still grasping

the concept of releasing pain

in the form of mental ashes...

as I exhibit my faith in you through

crying tears of gasoline

while chewing on a book of matches...

My love life has been suffering

from much emotional starvation,

but I thank your soul and spirit

for ending this drought like segregation,

although you and I have never conversed on this level

I am grateful for your patience,

no longer in fear but rather fully prepared

to be in your acquaintance.

Our paths have crossed in several dreams

and you've grown in my mind ever since,

artistically I've taken pleasure in tracing your foot prints,

our conversations were purposeful and of long duration,

breath never shortened, stanza's never to be indented,

as if cupid has written the preface of our love

titled, "A lost love legacy now cemented."

Roses are Read

So I must admit, it was I who anonymously

wrote you those love letters in the forms of poems,

hoping you would recognize my writing style

and complement the empty side of my hearts throne...

Thank you for finally revealing yourself to me,

alphabetized love, A love that is destined to B,

C the way reality has linked us through memory,

releasing smoke signals from heavens chimney,

I spoke to U several times in coded calligraphy,

As I now confess, I'm finally ready to know your name...

Timothy G. Green

Kinship to Heaven

Roses are Read

In the eye of the sky clouds fervently cry,

Tearful remnants form prayerful imprints…

Images of my future home are outlined as a divine oasis,

My thirst for life is no longer hungered like a fetus; tasteless…

A vision of sitting atop the descending

sun has my mind so anxious,

that I must emotionally step back and retract

while instructing my soul to breathe easy.

The winds thrust a brawny gust as I voluntarily inhale,

I raise my hands high, closing my eyes,

while stretching my fingers wide

In order to coincide with my mind being blind;

to embrace this sacred Braille.

The clouds release tears of joy in aspiration;

So rightfully I kneel in honor,

in awe of this spiritual awakening...

Timothy G. Green

Deaf to the World...
hearing Heaven call

Roses are Read

The rhythms of my mannerisms fold
precisely like a dinner napkin,
soothing any heartache anxieties you may have
with the strength of aspirin,
during this season is your mind willing to imagine,
a lifetime of romance
that breathes the esteemed breath of a dragon?

The same breath that keeps your souls candle lit,
the same breath that restrains death in our relationship
to ever convict or exist,
the same breath that allowed my spirit to depict,
a sanctified righteousness in our love life manuscript,
imperative to our longevity is this key element...

Would you be so kind to massage my prides canvas?
If so, I shall comply by softly kissing all wounds
upon your heart until they vanish,
poising my lips with His words to heal its damage,
poising my lips with His words to seal its bandage.

After He I am your provider and your shelter,
Yet, I am wise enough to know that when
our trials begin to swelter,
that by faith we shall call upon His cherubs to be our helpers.

Timothy G. Green

Dismay shall come plenty of days as our opinions differ,

Unto you, Father God, I promise to always seek

common ground with her,

praying my love shall never fall like a leaf,

let alone grow weary and whither.

This shall birth our love to an undying distinction,

for it will be cementing our loves truest intentions,

of being everlasting...

Love, the watered down version

Timothy G. Green

Admittedly I'm reaching for love, will it reach back?

If I am fortunate enough to spot love, will it peak back?

If I am honored to ever greet love, will it speak back?

But if I falter and cheat love, will it retract?

May hope keep you afloat from drowning in my tears…

Yet, grant you serenity as you submerge deep

within the depths of depression,

during this unbalanced stage my manhood seems

to lessen as life teaches a lesson,

of suicidal thoughts with a distorted flow,

stagnated in a lonely puddle reflection...

Of tasting loves buffet my appetite is a virgin,

Forever a victim of hopelessness seems

to be my hearts excursion,

for I'm prone to drink "til I'm drunken

from love, the watered down version...

Will you...

Despite being a man who claims his

faults and many short comings,

I have utmost respect unto God for the creation of a woman,

I apologize on behalf of "we"

for whispering so many sweet nothings,

and neglecting to respect karma along

with her riveting repercussions,

apologies are due for our many sinful acts of lusting,

an evident factor of the many relationships I rushed in.

Will you...

Understand that I would have fought with my sword

for your every cause if,

God had perfected me personally with His

chisel and deemed me flawless,

I have always been two steps behind your Fall

stuck in August,

and apologize for the many times, unto your soul, I exhausted...

by not proceeding with our love in a manner more cautious.

I apologize for breaking the alignment of our trust

by not standing adjacent,

I apologize as a collective for those of "we"

who started to build families

but like cowards abandoned the roots of their foundations,

Roses are Read

selfishly replacing arrogance for the

humble tone of being complacent,

not accepting responsibility for the beloved

children "we" are defacing,

only adding fuel to the fire of the "broken family" nation,

from accountability running, eluding it evasive,

while speaking to you with threatening words

so abusive and flagrant

during every disagreement and altercation.

When the world gives me their back will you also deface me?

Will you abandon our trust and seek to replace me?

Or, will you glide your wings ever so safely,

into my hearts atmosphere and embrace me?

If my spirit were to weaken would your faith increase me?

If I pledge to stand over the edge of manhood,

would you release me?

If I were to even engage in this outer

life experience only briefly,

would you sow half of your soul to my soul,

upon my return to earth and complete me?

Are you willing to compliment my tears

of salt with your tears of vinegar?

Are you willing to revive my heart

when it turns frigid and adjust its temperature?
Can these acts of your love be selflessly administered?

When I am covered in shame will your
tears of prayers rinse me?
If they do shower me, will they empower me
and of your love convince me?
Or will you hold my acknowledgment of my faults against me?
Intensely, I pray you will accept my individuality for what it is
and dare not try to reinvent me...

Will you...

Partake in a relationship with me
if I vow to have all lust forbidden?
I would honorably request cupid to be our souls' proprietor
by having this oath, in His name, copy written;
I swear to you that from my hearts shadows
these words have arisen,
no longer knotted but instead laced in love
reminiscent of a ribbon,
whether or not you grant me this opportunity of loving
you is solely your decision,
"weather" or not you see past the turbulent
storms of my prior heartaches
is solely based upon your willingness to

Roses are Read

align it with your soul's vision...

Will you...

Never again strike my face with your nails

and use it as a scratching pad,

and dare me to hit you back

especially those of "we" who are on probation

and freedom is all "we" have,

Will you... please try to refrain from

comparing me to my father

through labeling me as a deadbeat dad,

and instead teach me to understand

how to walk on the proper parental path,

when I cry, it's through remorse,

yet you taunt "we" and laugh...

Why?

Love, on my knee I plea that you will accept this apology

on behalf of "we" who have struck you with brutal force,

for the many times "we" embedded in your mind that you were

worthless and next to nothing

as "we" blew out your self confidence torch.

I stand here in regret thinking of the cowardly way "we" often

put you and our children out on the porch,

and the ignorant audacity "we" had to spit in your face

with little or no remorse...

Even the many women "we" slept with knowing

how immoral it was

on the verge of destroying your pride,

and the times eyes looked you straight

in the face and confidently lied,

while claiming you to be "our" rose

yet being the hindering thorn on your side...

Ignorantly wishing you to damnation

out of ignorance and sheer frustration;

screaming how much happier we would be if you were to die,

I know these words may not persuade you,

thus, I'm praying you will view my new

found actions as positive steps

towards proving the authenticity of this outcry...

Perhaps when you hear my soulful remnants

coughing in my casket, or should I say coffin,

then in my unperfected realm of love you'll get lost in,

Will you...

Allow the armor protecting your heart to dampen

with my tears and soften?

Roses are Read

A plea unto thee that I have cried often...

However, I am on the rise to strengthening self
while heading in His direction,
wavering out the distorted puddle which streams my life
through an altered reflection,
thus I have admitted to your soul my many
Soulful Imperfections.

Will you...

Allow your wings to broaden and freely spread,
will your heart feed me selflessly
and gently allow my soul to be breast-fed?

When I struggle to stand and you see a tremble in my hands,
when you confuse His words released from my mouth
and accuse them of being "my" demands,
when my self esteem lacks and slowly slips into depression,
are you willing to offer your heart on the front line
to serve as my spirits protection?

Truthfully speaking, when my heart is weakened,
can I rightfully turn to you as my confidant
in search of positive light and uplifting from you,
my beloved spiritual beacon,

as my tears deepen from long suffering

after a full night of weeping?

Sweetheart, I will not scribe and pretend,

my lungs are losing in this race with the wind,

my breath control is unsteady,

my heart is pounding in my chest so heavy,

suicide often seems like the best option,

in myself I'm ready to completely box in,

sort of like a coffin...

miserably chaotic are the emotions

that I find myself uncontrollably lost in...

...Only to awaken to a promise of God's

that shall not be forsaken,

to you, the love of my life, you are not lightly taken,

even when I'm on the verge of breaking...

When you and I are not on the same accord

and clearly not relating,

I try and choose my words wisely against the will of Satan,

because your faith in me gives me daily inspiration.

Your faith in me gives me daily inspiration,

so I promise to try and choose my words wisely

against the will of Satan,

especially when we are not on one accord

and clearly are not relating,

Roses are Read

even when my trust is torn and on the verge of breaking,

I will continually thank God for you, precious love of my life,

and pray that you know lightly you shall never be taken,

so blessed am I daily for the opportunity to awaken,

to you my angelic song bird and God's promises

for our marriage that shall not be forsaken...

It's like a coffin, all opposite, deathly and chaotic emotions

I'll gladly toss in,

I promise to lean on the Lord whenever

suicidal thoughts surface in my mind

and try to become an option,

instead I'll trust His word by dismantling these thoughts,

in a display of faith via spiritually shadow boxing.

Acknowledging you as my heart means

I can pound my chest heavy,

allowing love to guide my words so I breathe with ease steady,

finding no reason or motive to pretend,

so I swear to give God my utmost praise, as I thank Him,

for allowing my lungs to be winning

this race against spiteful winds...

Longsuffering will lead to trusting as I endure nightly weeping,

I promise to begin to speak life into my tears

when they begin to deepen,

every time they touch my cheek,

I will seek you my spiritual beacon,

and RIGHTfully so because my heart

will never turn LEFT to you, beloved confidant,

with God's help you will continue to comfort me

during the times when my spirit is weakened.

So I thank you for standing in the front line for my heart

in the form of protection,

for positively impacting my self esteem when it lacks

and slowly seems as if it is headed to

becoming a prey of depression...

Even when you seek Ye first and know that

my words released are not "my" demands...

I thank you for lifting me when I struggle to stand,

as your touch comforts every tremble found in my hands.

Gently you continue to allow my soul to be breast-fed,

I am humbled as your heart feeds me selflessly,

and cherish the portrait you continue to paint every time

you allow your wings to broaden in He and proudly spread...

My love for you continues to grow

and shows no sign of condensing,

spiritually it is charged with authority and conviction,

rebuking every attack that comes against

us in the form of conflicting,

Roses are Read

healing our spirits from Satan's iniquities that are sickening,

for my love is rooted by God, thus its strength

is His jubilant rendition.

As long as we remain faithful my beloved Angel – He is able,

Liturgically continue to lift your praise unto Him,

Through the clapping of your hands

along with the ordered steps of your ankles,

syrupy are my tears for our love, a glazed essence of maple...

Dear Lord, amongst your chosen I humbly

pray You consider her,

allow Your words to manifest upon her

tongue as rewarding literature,

allow not the ways of the world to deeply scar or whiter her,

nor the words of man to discourage her walk and hinder her,

thus of sin heavenly Father, may You continue to deliver her,

Deeper into Your will...

Allow her love to continue to orchestrate my hearts symphony,

so that Your blessings paint scripted messages

with powerful imagery,

that shall light our paths with lamps,

as we embrace our ministry,

cherishing these priceless moments

also known as sacred memories...

My God, may she and I forever outlast shame,

may Your grace merge our hearts so

that we always outcast blame,

I swear my loyalty to her with all my breath

and my hearts last flame,

I offer her my life and am willing

to die for her Heavenly Father,

As I claim the day she lovingly accepts my last name.

Loneliness will have been denounced once we are pronounced

husband and wife;

you will have accepted my Soulful Imperfections…

Well, future wife, will you?

About the Author

Timothy G. Green is an educator at heart. Aside from being a Program Coordinator, he also provides leadership workshops via poetry and motivational speaking to local community based organizations.

Roses are Read: Love lost or found is the first book being published through INKaissance Books in 2019. The 2nd book to be released through INKaissance Books this year is the critically acclaimed "Poetic Novel", 2nd Edition of *As A Child My Eyes Heard It First*. INKaissance will also be launching its Roses are Read artistic imprint this year.

He is a Christian and blessed husband to a beautiful wife and honored to be a father of a 13 year old daughter and a 6 year old son. He is also the proud founder of INKaissance. He continues to seek innovative ways to assist the Hartford community with leadership, social, and educational opportunities. Being recognized as a servant leader is a privilege that he doesn't underestimate nor under value.

Connect with Timothy G. Green.

> e-mail: inkaissance@gmail.com

> Facebook: Timothy G. Green

> Instagram: timothy_inkaissance_green

www.ingramcontent.com/pod-product-compliance
Lightning Source LLC
Chambersburg PA
CBHW072232190626
46809CB00017B/1848